Hi! I'm the bus driver. Listen, I've got to leave for a little while, so can you watch things for me until I get back? Thanks. Oh, and remember:

Don't Let the Pigeon Drive the Bus!

words and pictures by mo willems

WALKER BOOKS
AND SUBSIDIARIES
LONDON • BOSTON • SYDNEY • AUCKLAND

First published in Great Britain 2004 by Walker Books Ltd, 87 Vauxhall Walk, London SE11 5HJ

This edition published 2004

10 9 8 7 6 5

© 2003 Mo Willems

First published in the United States by Hyperion for Children

British publication rights arranged with Sheldon Fogelman Agency, Inc.

Printed in Singapore

British Library Cataloguing in Publication Data is available

www.walkerbooks.co.uk

for cheryl

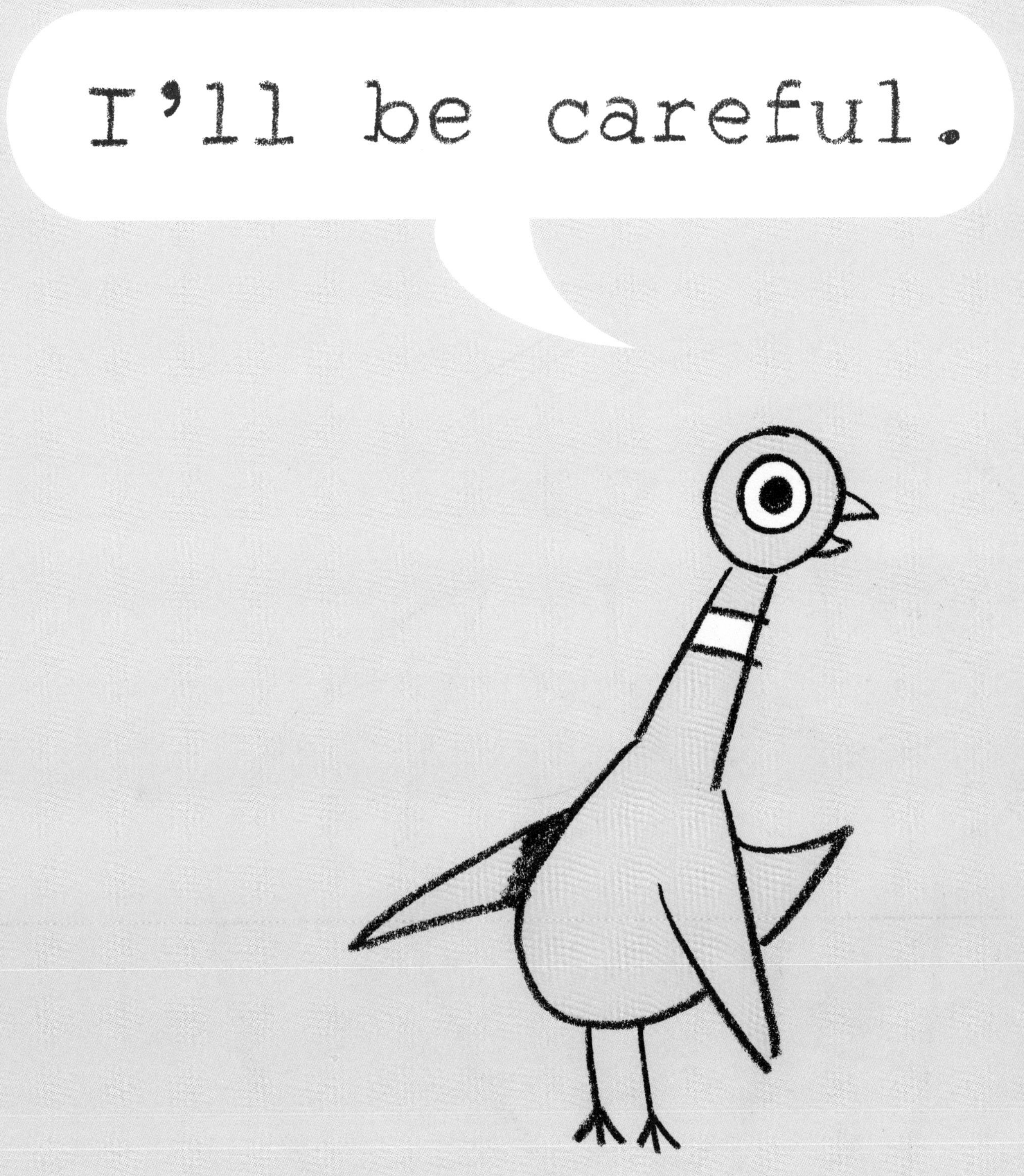
I'll be careful.

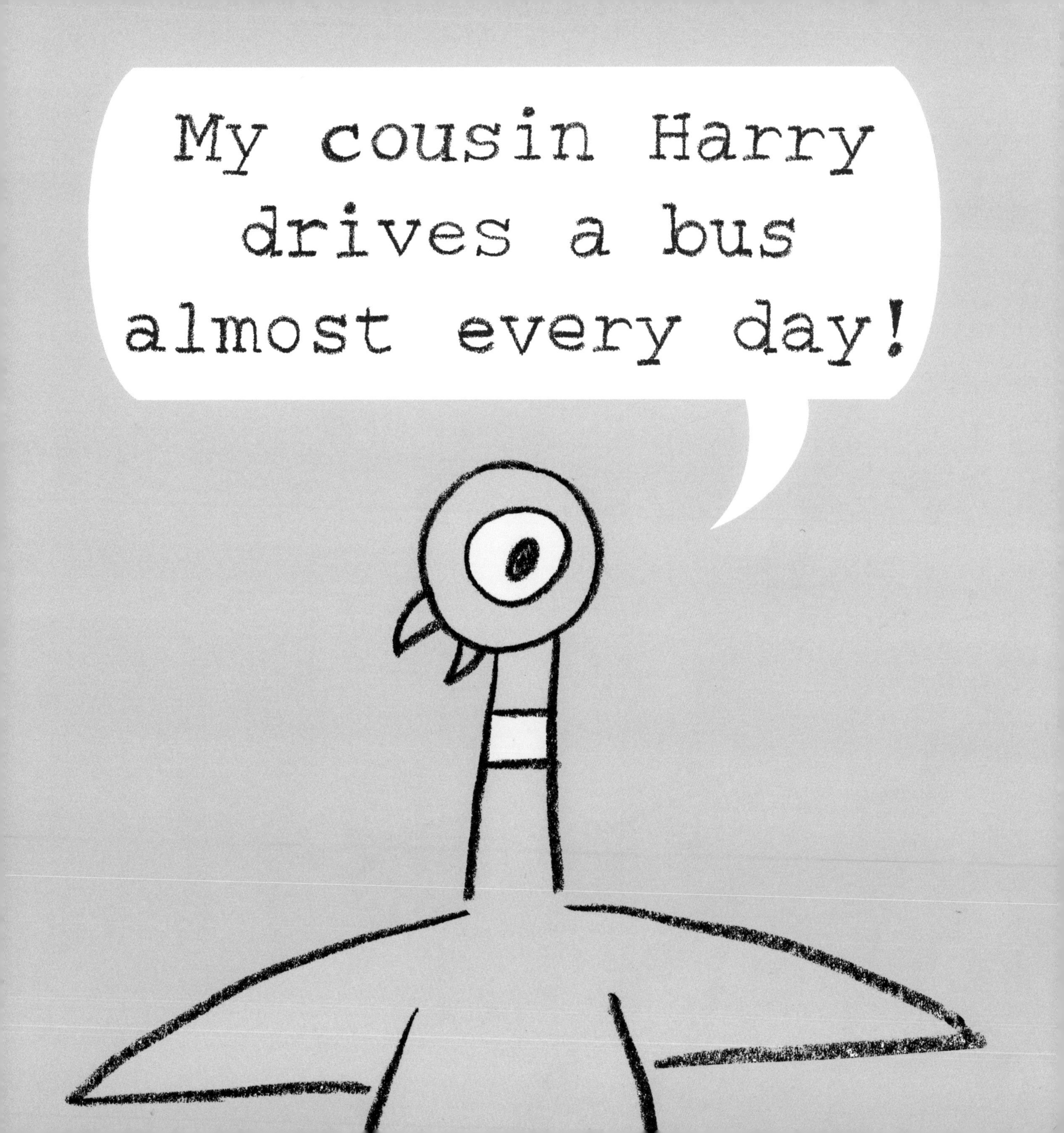
My cousin Harry drives a bus almost every day!

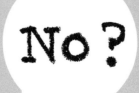

I'm back! You didn't let the pigeon drive the bus, did you?
Great! Thanks a lot.

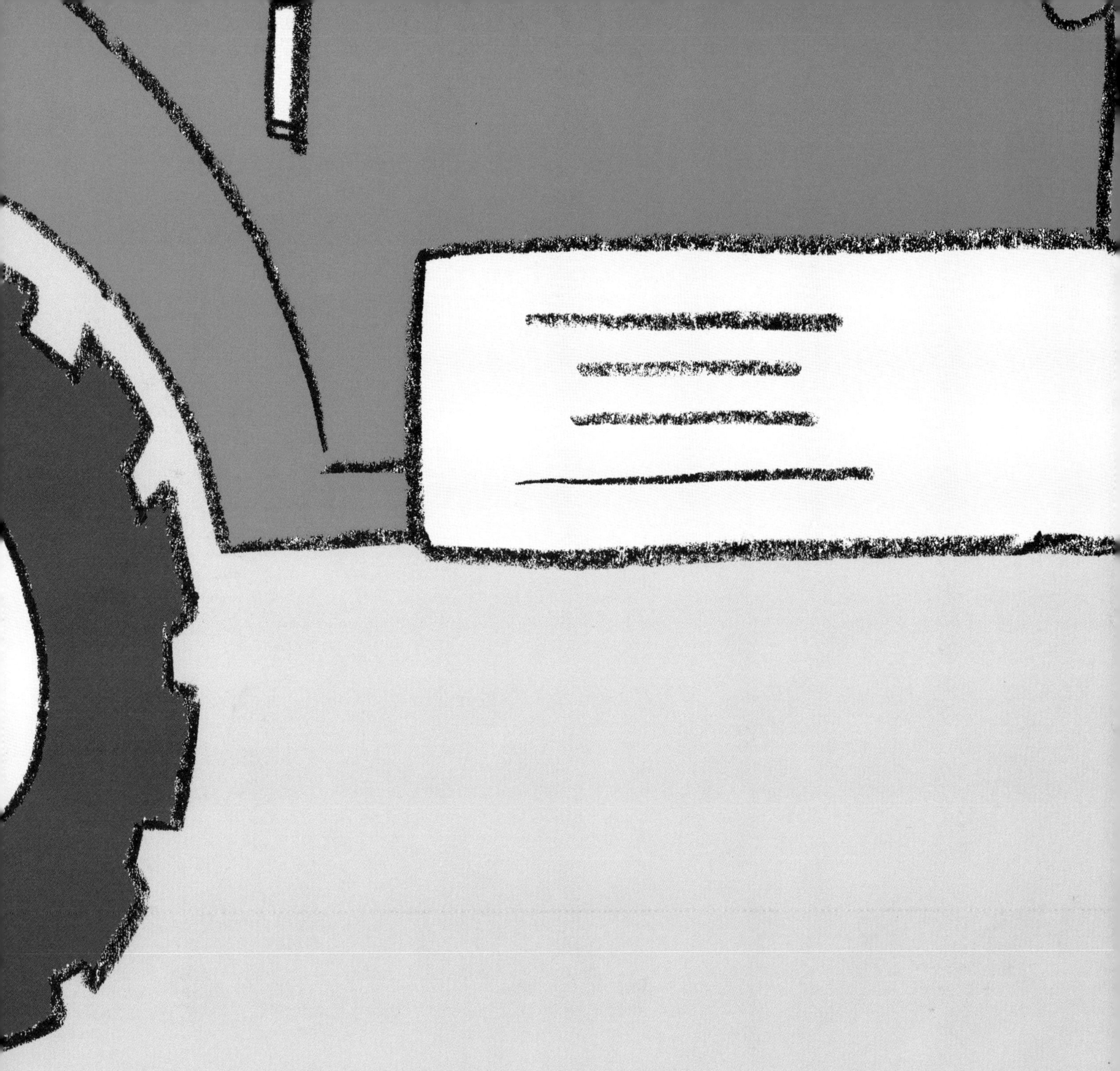

WALKER BOOKS is the world's leading
independent publisher of children's books.
Working with the best authors and illustrators
we create books for all ages, from babies
to teenagers – books your child will
grow up with and always remember. So…

FOR THE BEST CHILDREN'S BOOKS,
LOOK FOR THE BEAR